"A Lack of Writing Skill is a greater and greater handicap with every passing year."

Evincepub Publishing

Parijat Extension, Bilaspur, Chhattisgarh 495001
First Published by Evincepub Publishing 2021
Copyright © Neha Gupta 2021
All Rights Reserved.

ISBN: 978-93-90442-73-7

Writing in 21st Century

A COMPLETE SURVIVAL KIT FOR WRITERS

Neha Krishna

God, who looks after me and my family.

My parents and siblings, for always loving me UNCONDITIONALLY, no matter what, even amidst imperfections and tough stages of my life. I am immensely indebted to my parents, who believe in me, motivate me, respect my desires and ambitions and most importantly, empower me to believe in myself. If I am blessed to live long enough, I will try to be as good a mother to my daughter as you are and always have been to me.. Love you Mumma.. Love you Papa..

My husband, for being in my life. I need to mention my deepest sense of gratitude to my husband- Puneet, who tolerates all my tantrums as well as incessant disappearances into my work corner. Writing a book is harder than I thought and more rewarding than I could have ever imagined. None of this would have been possible without his support, who made sure to pepper me with encouragements and compliments, whenever I felt the blues. Although I'm intrinsically motivated, there are times I need to hear someone else's advice. Puneet has taught me a lot about being more organized with my thoughts and creating processes to execute day-to-day tasks. Yes, we've had our ups and downs, but they've been a blessing for us. Each time we've had it rough, we have experienced the meaninglessness of this life without each other.

All my students as well as colleagues, who actually gave me a line of thought to write this book. I owe an enormous debt of gratitude to all, who provided me different angles and lenses through which I could see the pattern of language development adopted by different learners. They gave me a variety of experiences through which I could actually analyze various degrees of apprehensions as well as difficulties faced by people during the process of writing.

All the people, I met during my travels and talks, who vehemently contributed in my continuous writing journey.

Finally, thanks to everyone at Evincepub.

Read, read, read. Read everything--trash, classics, good and bad, and see how they do it. Just like a carpenter who works as an apprentice and studies the master. Read! You'll absorb it. Then write. If it's good, you'll find out. If it's not, throw it out of the window."

--William Faulkner

(The quote itself suffices the message. Really if you want to become a writer you first need to dive into the world of books. The more you read the more you equip yourself with ideas. The more ideas you have the better content you'll produce through your writing. In addition, unconsciously you also get acquainted with the technique of writing.)

A Letter to the Reader

Thank you, dear reader, for picking up this book. This is my first non-fiction book, packed with all the essential tools to help you write unforgettable stories as well as impactful business documents. As the title of the book suggests, the book deals with writing in 21st century. Now what do I mean by that? Well, we all know that language changes. You and I don't speak or write the way Chaucer and Shakespeare did. Do we?

Not only the language but the way of expression, the mode of communication, the subject matter of novels, the premises of stories and thus the entire writing world has undergone a reasonable shift.

In 21st century, writers are way more social on online platforms and thus they get into the need of sharing ideas, updates and information with others more often. In this fast-moving world, it has become a necessity to write in a manner that should convey much more in the least possible words. People don't have the entire day to comprehend your mails full of jargons and at the same time the content written in a layman's language is considered as having no weight. So, it's important to learn how to strike that balance which makes your writing punchy and elegant.

Today's writer uses language and technology in surprising ways unlike past times. In this information ready world, where the information is just a click away, writer needs to be careful enough about the information he/she includes in his/her work. He/she needs to evaluate and fact check sources for truth and bias. Besides, today's writer also needs to be competent as well as creative enough to use that information wisely.

Today's writer, not only records his reflections privately in journals, but also publicly on blogs or other social media platforms.

Today's writer is well equipped with technology and is 24X7 supported by latest apps and tech trends to check for his grammatical errors and thus does not need to worry about that.

Apart from this, in this world full of distractions, if your story is not captivating enough, it will very easily be dumped. So, it becomes very important for your story to be woven with the warp and weft full of thrill/suspense/emotion so that the readers are spell-bound and thus, can't leave your work in the mid. Then only your work will be picked by this busy generation.

Thus, this book is a one-time investment for your ever-lasting success because no matter, you run a small business or occupy a small corner cubicle of a multinational corporation, chances are that the bulk of your job consists of communicating with others, most often in writing.

No one knows exactly how much poor communication costs business, industry and government each year, but estimates suggest billions. Poorly-worded emails, careless reading/listening to instructions, documents that go unread due to poor design or hastily presenting inaccurate information — all of these examples result in inevitable costs. The problem is that these costs aren't usually included on the corporate balance sheet at the end of each year, so often the problem remains unsolved.

Now to proceed towards the solution, go ahead and read this book to become a **PRO** at writing captivating stories as well as business documents.

Content

"Start writing, no matter what. The water does not flow until the faucet is turned on."

— Louis L'Amour

STORY WRITING

I

THE BASIC OUTLINE

The first thing, to focus, is the basic structure/outline of your story. Everyone in the world is gifted with huge imagination and so are you. Just the thing is that we never intend to pen our ideas down on paper. And until it's on paper, in a couple of hours, the ideas find their ways back to their own world. We need to pen it down on paper for it to breathe life.

It's very important to have a 'Glossary' of your own ideas which will surely amaze you when you'll turn back the pages and read your own ideas years later. So, finally you have to analyze your ideas and discover the genre of your expertise. Like for me, fantasy is the most interesting genre as I am a kind of person who enjoys living in her own Fantasyland.

So, find out what's your genre, no doubt that you can write all the genres once you sit back to write but, just as we have multiple and specific Intelligence domains, we can be good at multiple things but we would surely be best at some specific areas. So, just pen down your ideas and filter your own ideas by reading those ideas as a reader, there will surely be few outstanding ideas which may be anchored upon to develop and start writing.

If you feel more inclined towards adventures, you will surely want to write something about either your own trip to any such places or would try your hands on your dream journey to such places. There are times, when we feel so enchanted by the piousness of a place or a person that we strongly feel like composing few lyrical lines/hymns. Few amongst you must be sitting in your balcony, enjoying the warmth of a hot mug of coffee and reading this book, waiting to witness the splendid sunset. So, why don't you start writing with me about your experience along with vivid description of this natural sight!

Many of you must be now thinking about how to start, how to develop your story and finally how to conclude it. Let's start with a few suggestions on this- The basic structure goes like this-

Story Writing

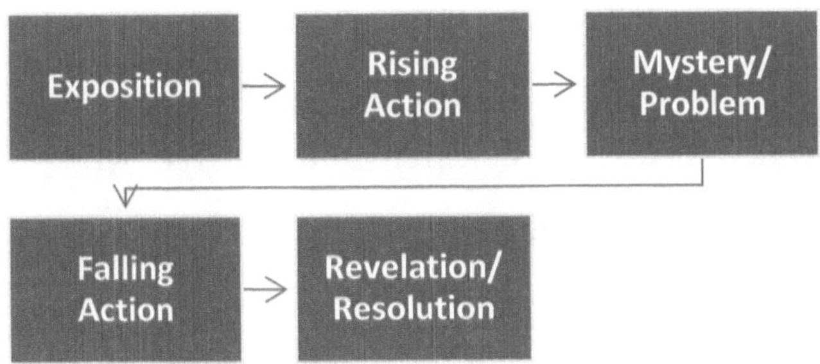

This process can very well be anchored upon if you are a beginner, once you get comfortable with it, you can for sure enjoy a little bit of deviation like most of my stories start with nail-biting scene (climax/mystery/problem). What about starting your story with a normal daily routine kind of character waking up a morning only to find that he's the only creature left on the Earth... After all, writing is nothing but a spontaneous flow of imagination/thoughts, structured with some set patterns and these patterns need to be flexible to provide you the freedom of expression.

Let's start with understanding story writing-

Just like before we start cooking, we get all the ingredients ready at our disposal, to write a story we first need to have the following elements ready-

- A Setting/plot
- Theme

- Characters
- A problem/ Mystery
- Solution/ Revelation

To remember these elements one can read the word 'STORY 'as an Acronym for the following-

S - Setting/plot

T - Talking characters

O - Oops a Problem

R - Resolution/Revelation

Y - Yippie… I did it

So, first be ready with your storyline setting like

- When and where will the incidents take place?
- Will it be a dynamic story covering many places or will it confine itself to a single setting?

Now let's decide upon the characters…

- Choose a protagonist.
- Choose secondary or supporting characters.
- There needs to be a hero and a villain. You may even have some characters supporting the hero and the villain.

There has to be some surprise elements/tragic stage/problem/suspense depending on your storyline.

If you are not intending to write a sequel of your story, you should reveal the mystery/resolve the problem by the end.

That's all what you require to start your story. Now to go step by step, first you need to start your story with an interesting **exposition** where you need to introduce your main characters, supporting characters, the setting of your story as well as your plot to your readers. Proceeding towards the climax, now you need to develop your story, which is known as **rising action**. This is the moment when you need to add a few setbacks. If you intend to write a full-fledged story, you must need to add sub-plots too.

Once you have reached the final **climax**, this is what is the peak of your story. Here, the antagonist becomes so powerful that it becomes very difficult

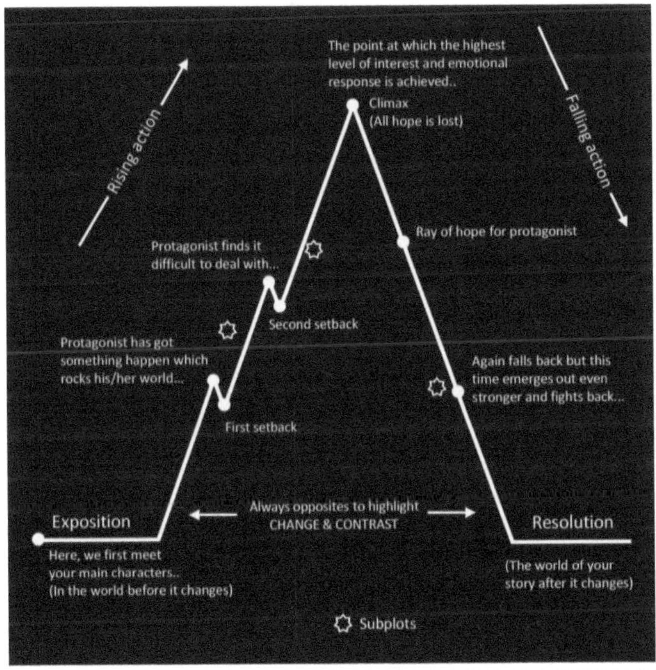

for the protagonist to survive. Now, you need to descend from this peak by gradually unfolding the layers of the mystery or by resolving the problem. This is what we call **falling action**. The protagonist finds a silver lining amid the dark clouds. Finally, the story should come to an end by providing the reader full contentment through **revelation /resolution.**

No tears in the writer, no tears in the reader. No surprise in the writer, no surprise in the reader."

—Robert Frost

II

THINK THROUGH SENSES (NOT ONLY FIVE BUT ALL SIX SENSES)

Whatever and wherever you are writing, try to include all your senses -

- What you can see
- What you can smell
- What you can hear
- What you can taste
- What you can feel
- What you can sense

These tips will come to your rescue whenever you'll be left with the only choice of repetition to meet the word limit for your exam. Also, if you want your story to come alive when read by your reader, you must include your senses.

Actually, this is the way to completely indulge into your story. But you need to keep one thing in mind that only the main character, from whose point of view you are writing your story, can describe these things in detail like let say you are writing in first person narrative then you'll **only** write what **YOU** can see, hear, taste, smell, feel or sense. You can't write "*The person sitting next to me in the park could feel the warmth of the iron bench due to the hot weather.*"

To understand it in detail let us take a natural setting.

If you are sitting in your balcony, enjoying the soft downpour……

You can describe the tiny droplets falling from the thorn-like edge of the leaf or dozens of droplets falling on the rusty black railing of your balcony or the happy faces of students returning half way after getting the news of Rainy-day, people with colorful umbrellas running with utmost care so as not to slip on the muddy road and whatever you can see.

It can be anything that a reader can easily relate to. You can describe the pitter-patter of rain, the sharp sound of raindrops on a tin-shade of that little tea-stall, the oozing of breeze, the thundering or even the voice of your Mumma, coming from the room being fussy about how easily you discarded the responsible thought of bringing the clothes (hanging on the rope) back in the room. What about the earthy smell! Anybody on the Earth can relate to it. Equally strong is the muggy smell of the rooms, because of the dampness usually when it's been raining since last few days. Why not to add the smell of burning oil and getting the taste of those oily onion fritters, much before getting them physically on a platter served before you. These are just few examples to get you on the track. At this point of time, you won't even realize how strongly would you impact the reader by just adding one liner description of your sense of touch like- *"cool breeze gave me a heavenly pleasure to feel the warmth of the hot mug of coffee between my palms."*

Don't underestimate the impact of your sixth sense on the scene. It doesn't need to be a highly intellectual one. Even your slight insight over the circumstance would do wonders. Like you can add how your blurred thought of getting a guest turned into reality within just a couple of minutes. Or how you were quite nostalgic with faded memory of your childhood days, when you always loved to ride bicycle in rains and suddenly your son came running with a request to allow him go out in rain to ride his tricycle.

Dear reader, you do not need to add all these expressions in your writing. Remember excess of anything is not good. It will bore your reader. Use it in moderation and your writing will be cherished.

———

GENERATE RESPONSE FROM YOUR READERS

Your story should not simply record your feelings or opinions, rather it should generate response into your readers' mind and heart.

For ex- My brother is multi-talented. (Makes your readers passive readers)

Whereas, if you write few sentences like-

My brother is a great photographer.

My brother is truly a chef.

My brother is an Interior Designer by profession.

The most probable responses your readers will have to it -

- Oh my god, what a great variety of skills he has.
- He must be a gifted man.

- Oh! how fondly I wished I could be a photographer.

Or even more than this. The point is that you need your readers to generate their own responses rather than just reading with their brain shut.

Here you need to be extra conscious when you are writing a persuasive piece because in that case you need to drive your readers' mind as per your requirement. Thus, you need to draft your cues accordingly. After all, the responses generated by the readers will lead to their agreement or disagreement towards your view point.

"I kept always two books in my pocket, one to read, one to write in."

--Robert Louis Stevenson

IV

PRO AT DESCRIPTION

Now see if you really want to be good at describing, you need to be good at observing your surroundings. No matter where you are or what you are doing, make sure that you are cognizant of your surroundings. Whatever noise you are hearing, try to find a word to suit that noise like if you get to hear the vroom-vroom of engine, or the shrill noise of a drilling machine or may be the raucous sound of something, you need to know the specific words to describe all those sounds.

Similarly, if you witness the hustle bustle of a narrow street full of vegetable vendors, buyers as well as few stray animals feeding upon the peels thrown on the road, you need to have the describing words to describe the scene. Make sure that your description should be strong enough to enable your readers visualize the scene. And that is when, the reader will find himself a place in your story.

Once you'll be conscious over your need of getting to know the exact words to describe, you'll be better observer as well as writer.

Try to observe even the minute details like how the aunty of your neighborhood keeps giving the daily news broadcast to your mother from her balcony. Focus on her expression, how she frowns while telling about the guy, who is a criminal for her just because he has long hair and wears a silver earring. Try to overhear the conversations between people. You can even get some clues by overhearing casual phone conversations. You never know which trivial incident might leave you with an excellent idea to start your story with.

Even the fat stout lady, sitting and snoring with her mouth wide open beside you in a crowded bus, will give you great deal of details to add in your description to infuse life into your character.

A super modern girl with contoured make up talking on phone with her friend using 80% of modern slang may give you a good sum of words if you want to write about modern teenage relationships.

The description should be so strong and powerful that the reader can visualize the character or the scene. Let us discuss about describing scene in detail.

Scene is the series of actions occurring one after the other. There are leading scenes as well as supporting scenes. Leading scenes are the scenes, which lead to the climax, and supporting scenes help to develop your characters.

If you want your scenes to be so powerful and realistic that the readers start visualizing the scenes, as they go through the lines, then try to add snippets of natural phenomena into your description. Read the following description to understand better-

- *"My home town, known as pink town, was really once a town of pink brick, it would have been pink if the smoke and ashes had allowed it.…"*
- *"As the train passed, a sudden shock of a great earthquake caused everything falling and breaking. But, the breaking of the Vase created a kind of melodramatic silence in the drawing room. Everyone was in awe.…"*

Thus, you can create magic through your vivid description.

V

CHARACTERIZATION

Ok my dear reader, let's now get familiar with the characters of the story. Plainly speaking, the characters of the story should be like you and me. When I say you and me, it's clear that the characters should be real life characters and not so saint-like character like the mythological figures. This is because, the readers like the characters who they can relate with. Have you ever seen your mothers or grandmothers crying over the plight of homely kind of character of daily soap serials? It's a very common sight at homes, isn't it? So why does that happen... because somewhere at the back of their mind and heart, they start relating with the characters and thus, engage themselves very spontaneously with the storyline.

Many a times, we feel empathetic towards something which we think that we do not relate to at all. Why? Actually, there are a number of feelings, memories as well as emotions which sometimes knowingly but most of the times unknowingly are suppressed deep within our unconscious memory. Several studies even go on to the extent of saying that the dreams we see at night are also the manifestation of it.

What I want you to understand here, is that the characters who are like you and me gain more sympathy and affection by us. Because, deep inside our hearts, there are always few regrets, few guilts, fears or sometimes even anguish or frustration which we rarely get a chance to speak out. These emotions most of the time don't even get the privilege of getting translated into our thoughts because we get hurt even by thinking about such things. In these cases, reading something similar provides relief to us. And mentally we feel more stable.

Thus, as a writer, it becomes our responsibility to provide that relief to the readers.

Okay, so on this note, I would take you to the aspect of character building, i.e. **How to infuse life into your characters?**

For any character to come alive, it should be able to think, feel, act and desire. Let us dig deeper-

Thinking Chord- What is the basic thinking thread of your character? What is his ideology? For example- There are many people in this world who believe in God and their ideology is – 'God sees everything' so the story of this character will be entirely different from that of the character whose ideology is – 'Everything in this galaxy is driven by Scientific Principles'. You character might even be of materialistic bent of mind whose basic thinking thread might be – 'Money can buy anything'. You can even create a character who is lovesick and thinks that 'Love is eternal'. So, find out what is the main ideology your character believes in.

Feeling Chord- If you look around, there are variety of people, some people always seem happy, they are always lively and cheerful so their base feeling is 'Happiness'. Some are always gloomy, no matter what happens, after few hours, they'll come back to their base emotion i.e. sadness. Many a times, we associate few words like grumpy, angry young man etc. to certain people because they are mostly seen shouting and fussing about things, so their base feeling is 'Anger'. Sometimes we come across people who look very peaceful and calm and we get positive energy when we meet them so their base feeling is 'Calmness'.

So, there are thousands of feelings. Try to find out what is the feeling chord, you have chosen for your character.

Activity Chord- You character needs to have a set of key activities. For instance- if your character is a homemaker, his/her key activities are household chores. The activity chord of a Scientist is conducting experiments. So, you need to, here and there, show your characters' key activities throughout your storyline to infuse life-like characteristics in your characters.

Desire Chord- Now, this chord needs to be very active throughout your storyline. This is the motivation that drives your character to act. It can be good or evil, it can be anything based on the theme of your story. For example- your character might be desirous of marrying his/her love, taking revenge of his/her friend's murder, or regaining his/her lost identity.

So, this is entire process of creating your character and infusing life into it.

VI

DIALOGUES/SOLILOQUY

To give your story a theatre or movie like effect, you need to add few dialogues here and there. Soliloquy facilitates us express our mental dilemmas or aggression. In case, if you want to make your story even more impactful, you can also add few monologue statements. Read these dialogues-

"A (furiously) - What the hell is this! Don't tell me that you have lost it.

B (hesitantly) - Actually, I...I.....I didn't lose it but.. it got lost on its own...

A (violently) - As if it had wings.. I'll just kill you.."

See as you read the words given under the brackets, your tone of subvocalization (internal speech typically made while reading) gets changed accordingly. Thus, you get the exact idea of the story.

Now look at the other one-

I, irritated by him, couldn't do anything but muttered to myself "I'm gonna kill this man, what does he think of himself, I am way better than hundreds of him" despite the fact that he could anytime crush me like a mosquito.

Thus, you can create the whole of theatre through your writing by using dialogues, monologues and soliloquy.

———⌁———

VII

PROBLEMS/SUSPENSE

Dear reader, if you want your readers to cling to your writing from starting till end, you certainly need to weave your story around an intense mystery or problem. In the beginning or prologue of your story, just give your readers a pinch of spice in form of clue what it's going to reveal by the end. Like-

Tia (so tensed) - So, tell me.. why again??

Me (Almost in tears) - ….because I can't take it anymore, I want to end it all. I want to die. I...

Tia(in a curt manner, cutting me short)- No, you don't, You don't want to die. Do you get that.. You DON'T want to die, Keshav. Actually, you can't die...

Me (furiously)- Yes, I want to die and that is why I jumped into the river but those bunch of crooks, I don't understand why do these people make it the sole purpose of their lives to save the lives of others. Why couldn't they just let me die. I must say they ......

Tia- Oh please... They saved you because you cried for help, You Moron... if you really wanted to commit suicide, why the hell did you shout...? See I am telling you... stop doing this time and again...

And this is how my mental state has taken a toll on me. I myself can't figure out what I am up to. And the whole world around me has suddenly come into the action to preach me about the importance of life. Where were all these people at the time when I wanted to live my life, when I was super excited with what I had and this cruel world seemed to be so skeptical about how can a guy of 26 be so successful as well as happy guy on the Earth. Why didn't they let me do what I wanted...

That's all... you just need to arouse curiosity in the minds of your readers to know more about your story. Now let the readers get engrossed into the world of Keshav till the last page.

Now, you have the full freedom to start your story from the mid and then go back into flashback or start the story since the beginning. Trust me, both work superfine. Just make sure that whatever phase you start with, you need to get your readers dive into it.

Now, I recommend my dear readers to create the problem/mystery very carefully because it makes the climax. The problems are the highest peak of your story, if it is weak, you'll lose your readers. The problem/mystery should be such that the readers are not very easily able to guess or foresee its resolution/revelation. Thus, the climax has the sole responsibility to keep your readers glued till the end.

So, try to create problem which is coming to your protagonist like a bullet or a cyclone which is going to rock his/her world so badly that he/she is left with no other option than to fight with it.

Try to weave your suspense in such a way that your reader keeps entering into a tunnel slowly and slowly and finally when you are successfully able to place your reader at the darkest spot of the tunnel, he/she can do nothing but continue reading until he finds a way out. Here, why I took tunnel to explain because I wanted to draw a comparison between tunnel and story.

Imagine you are at the darkest spot of a tunnel. All you can hear is your own footsteps. How will you come out of it? Obviously, you will keep on moving and at a point of time, you'll start getting a sort of hollow roar ahead, a kind of faded light, which gives you an idea that you are about to come out and then gradually the voice gets louder and louder and finally you come out.

This is how you need to reveal the mystery.

It should not be that from the summit i.e. the climax, you make your reader plummet.

———∽∾———

VIII

CLIFF-HANGING ENDING

Now, if you have plans to write a sequel you should learn the art of leaving your first part of story at a Cliff-Hanging state. Even those, who intend to write weekly columns, need to learn this. Your story should end at a point where the reader is left anxious to know about the further course of action just like the web series or daily soaps do. Look at the given example-

Madly in love with Danny, Manisha had no idea that Danny was no one else but the same grumpy colleague of hers whom she could never have even dreamt of dating even if he were the last creature on Earth. Same was the case with Danish who had no clue that Mini was no one else but the same arrogant girl who never missed a chance to humiliate or insult him in front of his friends.

Finally, these Insta love birds plan to meet each other in person. Sunday was the day decided for this catastrophic event to take place. Finally, Mini in her favourite black dress and highlighted curls rolling down all over her shoulders is waiting for Danny to arrive. Danny too enters the restaurant in his recently bought denim teamed up with black t-shirt just because black was Mini's favourite colour.......

Will they forget about their real-life grudges and go ahead with their internet love or will they uninstall Instagram from their phones and go on their ways never to meet them again…

So, this way the reader is left open to ponder over what is going to happen next and thus you hook you readers to read the sequel.

IX

RESOLUTION

As I spoke about the problems in the last section. I would reiterate one aspect that the problem/suspense of your story or what we term as climax of your story needs to be so powerful that the readers are encouraged to read ahead to know about the resolution/revelation.

Now what should be done to make your resolution equally powerful to satisfy your readers?

The solution should certainly have a great emotional touch in it. After all we human beings are filled with an ocean of emotions. If the final solution leaves the readers flooded with emotions, then your story is going to be remembered forever. Moreover, the final solution provided must involve life-threatening decisions and risks because it makes the readers empathize with the characters very strongly.

Words can be like X-rays if you use them properly--they'll go through anything. You read and you're pierced."

--Aldous Huxley, Brave New World

X

Hit The Nail With Specific Vocabulary

Now as I proceed, I must mention the importance of specific vocabulary here. See, many a times we get to hear people say the food was good, that guy is good, the weather was good, the workshop was good, the clown was good. Have you ever given it a thought that **How can a guy, a dish and even a clown be described with same adjective?**

So, here what I want you to ponder over is that why to use the same adjective for each and everything when we have so many adjectives. Like the dish can be lip-smacking, the guy can be considerate or may be amicable, the weather can be relaxing, the workshop can be informative and the clown can be funny. So, minimize the usage of general vocabulary and maximize the usage of specific vocabulary.

Here are few examples area-wise-

<u>**Ailments/problems**</u>-

Stop using the words like unwell. Instead give some in-depth knowledge of the problem your character is facing like

- If your character is unwell because he has gone through something heart-rending, you can use the word heart-broken, melancholic, etc.
- If your character is not feeling well because somewhere he is not happy about his present life and wants to reminisce his past times, so he is being nostalgic.
- If your character is not feeling well because of the long trip and feeling uneasy in stomach you can say he is feeling nauseous.
- If your character just can't stand huge gatherings or public places he may be described as claustrophobic. Or maybe, if he/she feels uneasy at heights, we can say acrophobic.
- Mentally retarded if he is slow at learning or keeping pace with the others of his age.
- Exhausted if he has been working day in day out to make his both ends meet.
- Throbbing headache or acute headache if your character had had a hangover.

The list is never-ending. The thing is that you need to ask yourself how is your character feeling and because of what, which will probe you even further to describe his/her condition in better words. It will also help you in writing about what you feel on your social networking sites.

Cooking

Many a times we feel like describing what we ate last night. It's the time of social-media. Before we start eating, we first feel the need to post all over our WhatsApp status, Facebook or Instagram stories that we are blessed with such a delicious meal no matter how bald it tastes. So, it has become almost a necessity to know how to describe anything on the Earth in a fancy manner.

You should also know the terms for various steps in the cooking process like blanching, stirring, roasting, flipping, baking, grilling, steaming etc., if your story is revolving around a cook/chef or even if it is about a guy who is passionate about cooking because that way you'll be able to do justice to his character. Now if you want to write about a person who is foodie or someone who needs at least 30 people to send an emoticon with tongue out, and 20 people to wish *Bon Appetite* and at least 10 people to really send him an appreciation letter for his yummy post before he starts his meal. Then you would surely find some idea through given examples-

- Velvety fresh smooth Kadhi(a chickpea and buttermilk curry) flavoured with curry leaves..

(contrary to the fact that it is a clever way of using up buttermilk that was not fresh any more. Masking the staleness with spices and giving it body with some sort of thickener.)

- I just can't resist myself from eating this hot steaming pav bhaji topped with melting cubes of butter, a few coriander leaves and lemon wedges.

Singing-

Try using these personalized comments/remarks and see the difference-

- Your voice directly reaches to heart.
- You have a good control over high notes.
- You conveyed the emotions within the lyrics well.
- Such a soulful voice!
- Your voice is mesmerizing and moving.
- I felt your words go through me as your voice echoed the feelings the songwriter had meant for the listener to feel.
- Listening to you was a transcending experience and I hope to hear much more in the future.
- Your voice soothes my heart!

You can use melodious, mesmerizing, ravishing, captivating, spellbinding, alluring, soul touching and other words in your compliments for a singer.

<u>**Dancing-**</u>

- Your steps are super fine and graceful.
- Your movements were in perfect sync with the essence of the music
- Very precise steps, put together so well.
- It has always been a pleasure to watch you perform.

Graceful, mesmerizing, synchronized, expressive, heart-touching, creative, exemplary, beautiful, alluring and flawless are some of the appreciation words and compliments that dancers would love to hear!

<u>**Photography-**</u>

- You have an eye for details.
- Loved the play of light and shadows in this picture.
- The way, you set your focus on the silhouette and highlight it, makes the entire view look so stunning.

Thus, with a little more attention, you'll be able to find the core of anything which actually touched your heart.

BUSINESS WRITING

"No matter how brilliant or innovative an idea may be, if it is not communicated clearly and promoted effectively to the right audience, it will not yield the expected result. This section introduces you to the key elements of professional writing to draft impactful workplace documents and presentations to meet a variety of requirements."

Business Writing

Just like you have now learnt how to describe someone or something in detail, you need to understand that this kind of figurative or musical lines do not suit business writing.

Business writings are meant to be plain, concise, clear and unambiguous.

The following four points will help you understand the requirements of a business writing-

Simplicity

Clarity

Elegance

Captivity

So, use as few words as possible and try to uncomplicate your ideas. Good business writings are always confused with full of jargons. While the exact opposite is true. You don't need to fill your writing with so many complicated ideas and jargons which in turn may cause great difficulty for the reader to comprehend it. It will not serve your purpose rather your writing will seem more of a pretentious writing than an intellectual one.

The sentences should be crisp and concise so as to deliver meaning in the least possible time. Look at the following example, which I had read somewhere and found so interesting-

The notion that a competitive workplace environment is commensurate with superior performance is, at best, dubious.

Ok now read it once again... Most of the people will take some time to understand this statement. What if we write it in the following way-

Workplace competition doesn't necessarily boost performance.

Won't it make a more comprehensive message? See, when we read or talk about something in a business environment, obviously we don't have the whole day to work on understanding a single letter. So, it becomes foremost priority to keep the letters/mails short and simple.

Let us go deep into Business Writing

Business writing consists of not only the technical materials like- manuals, proposals, documentation etc. but also deals with writings produced for many day-to-day business operations like- written correspondence, internal communications, media releases, reports, circulars etc.

Why are Technical communication skills important?

Because, business writing consists of the communication of specialized technical information, which in turn decides the smooth functioning as well as the growth of the business.

Be it any organization, most of the time of functioning demands one or the other form of writing like writing reports, letters, memos, proposals, presentations, correspondence with colleagues, managers, clients and many more. And if we analyze the system even deeper, those on the higher posts get into the need of writing even more.

A lack of writing skills is a greater and greater handicap with every passing year.

Investing some time to polish your writing skill can result in a significant improvement in your hire-ability as well as promotional prospects.

No one knows exactly how much poor communication costs business, industry and government each year, but estimates suggest billions. Poorly-worded emails, careless reading/listening to instructions, documents that go unread due to poor design or hastily presenting inaccurate information — all of these examples result in inevitable costs. The problem is that these costs aren't usually included on the corporate balance sheet at the end of each year, so often the problem remains unsolved.

Now to proceed towards the solution, the further chapters are to be attended to.

⸺⧁⧀⸻

I

KEY TO BEGINNING

Business writing in itself has a number of varieties. Thus, professional writings can take many forms, depending on the purpose and intended audience.

Now, how to decide upon which form will suit which purpose and whether the selected form is accessible and appealing for the intended audience, the writer needs to have a proper knowledge of the following two aspects-

1. **Approach**

2. **Rhetorical situations (audience, purpose, context)**

Approach

First thing to be kept in mind is that your writing should be **reader-centered/audience centered**. Being a technical writing, it comprises of the technical specifications as well as the instructions which are meant to be transacted to the target audience in a way that audience finds it accessible, user-friendly, clear, goal-oriented and most importantly, profitable.

Second thing to be focused here is to have **problem-solving approach**.

Most of the technical writings tend to accomplish one or the other problem-solving tasks. Whether you are doing work for a client, for your employer, with your team, or for someone else, you will typically use some sort of design process to tackle and solve the problem.

For example – The following design process can be followed as a plan to solve a problem-

Empathize – With your users

Define – Your users' needs, their problems, and your perceptions

Ideate - By challenging assumptions and creating ideas for innovative solutions

Prototype – to start creating solutions

Test – solutions

The emphasis here should be flexibility. The design process for a technical writing should not be meant for a strict compliance, to be followed in a chronological order. Rather, it should be iterative. A clearly-articulated design process provides you with a clear, step-by-step plan for finding the best solution for your situation. (more on that later under the heading- 'HOW')

Rhetoric Situation

The circumstances under which the communication has to take place is known as Rhetoric Situation. To understand it better think of 4W1H i.e. Who, whom, what, why and How.

So,

Who i.e. Who is writing? i.e. Writer that means none other than you.

Writer- You need to have a general understanding of who you are. What is your position in the organization, what are your motivations towards the current scenario, what is your previous knowledge about the concerned topic/problem.

Whom i.e. whom are you writing to? i.e. The reader or better your target audience.

Target Audience- Now, on this stage you need to do a proper **Audience analysis**. Who is your target audience? Ponder over the following questions-

Is it a single audience?

Are you dealing with a multiple audience?

Is your audience internal?

Is your audience external?

Is your audience senior than you?

Is your audience junior than you?

Is your audience lateral?

Is your audience your client/customer?

Is your audience your service provider?

Thus, any writing piece without a detailed knowledge of the intended audience would not be more than a vague writing.

Now having known that the business writings should always be reader or audience centered and not writer-centered, you now need to understand how to do it-

When we write a journal/diary writing we need to be writer centered because it's all about us. Even when in the mid of any seminar or lectures, we make notes, that is very much for our own benefit and thus, we use all the forms and styles which appeal to us. Depending on our interest and need we tend to include the things which facilitates us.

But, when it comes to workplace communication, we need to divert the focus to the audience. Now it seems tricky to understand the audience fully. But, by making an Empathy Map, you'll easily be able to do it.

What i.e. what is the main agenda? What is it that you are expected to write about. In a more specific term- Task analysis

Task Analysis-

The task at hand is to be understood in detail like what is to be focused on, what all terms or data are to be recorded in the writing. The correctness and relevance of the content becomes of utmost importance here. Obviously, it's important here to analyze deeper and deeper over what all needs to be communicated to your audience, but more important here is **to omit the content or information that your audience does NOT need to be explained**. Keep in mind that at workplaces, people have a limited time to accomplish more and thus, they will not at all enjoy your story.

Once you've understood your audience in depth, analyze the task at hand. What you intend to accomplish through this communication. There are various types of tasks like- writing memos, writing presentation material, advertising content, media release, reports of events, invitations, letter of grievance, letter of thanks, instructional manuals, specifications manuals, and many more.

The purpose of each of these writings is different and thus, the style, form, tone, vocabulary, everything needs to be chosen appropriately suiting the purpose.

Therefore, first you need to put your task under a category of purpose like-

Promotion of your product/service	
Problem-solving	
Record-keeping	
Persuade/convince	
Information based letters	
Gratitude Letter/email	
Grievance Letter/email	
Invitation Letter/email	
Promotion Letter/email	
………	
………	
………	

Thus, based on the type of business, you deal with the list which consists of different categories. Now, as you have put your task at hand into a relevant category, you are good to go.

After, analyzing the category, the next step is to start writing.

Why i.e. what is the purpose of your writing? What gave rise to the need of this writing task? More precisely- What's the purpose?

Purpose- Now, the purpose behind the need of writing is to be clearly stated. If we narrow down the commonly recorded purposes of a workplace writing we get the following six main purposes behind all business writings-

- To solve a problem
- To improve a situation
- To give /take information
- To complain
- To keep record
- To persuade

How i.e. In what ways are you going to get your purpose served?

So, having known all about the rhetoric situations, here comes the role of **Design Thinking.** which covers your audience analysis, task analysis as well as the purpose. (Read next chapter to understand it in detail)

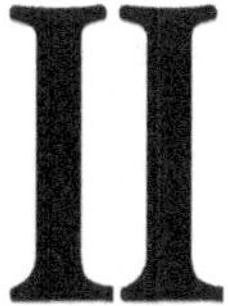

DESIGN THINKING

Design Thinking is an innovative problem-solving process which has several steps-

1. Empathize

2. Define

3. Ideate

4. Prototype

5. Test

Let's understand these steps in detail-

Empathize- Empathy Mapping is the core of Design Thinking. It is the best tool to empathize with the end users. This idea was first given by Dave Gray. So, Empathy Mapping or what I call it as getting into the brain and heart of your target audience. By using this tool, you get very close idea about the mental, physical as well as emotional state of your end user. You also come to empathize with the pain of your end user and what gain he/she desires for. Now, no matter if you have a single audience or multiple audience, you need to picture a specific audience in your mind.

Now let's take a case. We'll study a situation where you want to start a Daycare or play school. So, who will be your end user? A kid? Parent? Let's take one at a time. For giving you a clear idea on how to make an Empathy Map, let us try Empathy Mapping for this situation taking a child as our end user.

Basically, we need to think of the daily routine of that kid. Here you need to keep your eyes open, your ears open and most importantly your mind open while observing the kid.

Now just draw a human like figure in the center mentioning 'A Kid', or if you are working on MS Office, better to use an image of a kid which will help you picture him/her in your mind. Now draw lines as shown in picture what does the kid see, what does the kid hear, what does the kid say or do, what does the kid think or feel about.

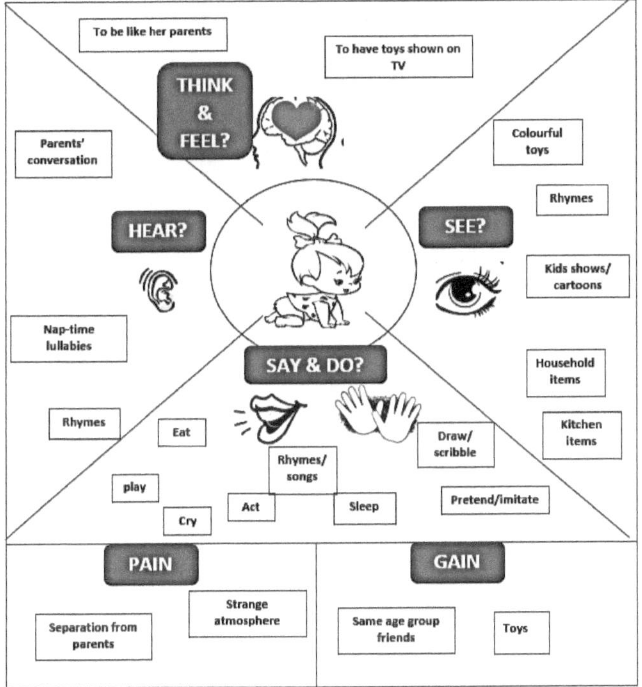

So, here you can see how we have to observe a kid very closely to complete this empathy mapping. In case if your end user is an adult, consider taking interview of him/her, and try to collect as much information about him/her as possible. This way your empathy mapping will be more authentic and useful.

Defining and Ideating

So, last chapter, we ended up making Empathy Map. Now, we'll see how to define and ideate the user's needs.

Definition should surely be clear but not only this will suffice, the key focus should be the needs of users and not only the aspirations of the profit makers.

Now let's suppose that the definition was this-

Let the design of the day-care serve as a flagship project for our company so that our existing goodwill and market value gets multiplied exponentially.

So, obviously if you have this goal in your mind, you'll provide best of the services and put in all your sincere efforts to meet the requirements of your end users.

What if the definition goes this way-

Let the design of the daycare be such that it aids and supplements the team to provide much better care and affection to the kids so that the kids' needs of finding love, care and security in absence of their parents are satisfied.

Won't this definition be more user centric because the shift is more towards the needs of the end users.

Now, as we have defined the problem, the next step is to brainstorm and ideate what all can be done to fulfil this goal. A number of ideas will come up here as a result of the data collection and Empathy mapping.

Analyze and synthesize the data in order to brainstorm and ideate.

For example, let us again take the same case and try to ideate-

- Let this be a double-storey building so as to have more rooms and kids are left with sufficient free space to play and explore.
- First of all, the furniture, the flooring, curtains, wall paints everything should be safe and free from hazardous chemicals to let the kids breathe fresh air.
- Bright colours are more liked by kids so let the rooms be colourful.
- As per our Empathy Mapping, we observed that few kids are used to of their mothers' lullaby when it comes to make them sleep, so how about having a good quality recording of the mothers' lullaby!
- As we analyzed that kids love to pretend and imitate different characters, let us create different areas to facilitate the kids in their role-plays like- a miniature doctor clinic area,

a miniature super market area, a miniature kitchen area and so on…

- Daily sanitization with disinfectant needs to be practiced given that the kids are prone to put things in mouth.

And so on and so forth….

Thus, we generate as many workable ideas as we can.

This step is termed as Ideation. Our next step which is Prototype will turn these theoretical ideas into action and thus, we'll come to know whether the ideas generated as of now will augur well or not.

It might be possible that few ideas don't at all work whereas few ideas need a bit of modification to make it work well. So, let us proceed with our fourth step...

———ᴄᴏᴏ———

Prototyping and Testing

Prototyping is creating a rough model to check whether the ideas generated at the end of Ideation step are really workable or not.

The model which you create should not be so expensive. So, finally when the ideas were worked upon, several findings came into light like-

- Hearing mothers' lullaby the kids were found searching for their mothers and thus our motto of making kids comfortable in the absence of mothers was failed badly so this idea was trashed out.

And so on…

So, by now we have completed four steps, now the last step is testing.

Again, taking the same case, following are the few facts which are revealed at this step-

- Two storey building didn't work well as the kids were found near the stairs which was quite risky so this idea was dropped.

And many more such facts can be revealed. Thus, this is how the Design Thinking helps in product designing, service designing, business designing as well as communication designing.

One thing, to be kept in mind here, is that this process is not linear, but it requires iteration as and when required.

30-20-50 WRITING

The writing process starts way before you start with your draft. There are a number of steps to write a clear, coherent and concise content. Let's discuss these steps

1. Planning- You should spend 30% of your writing time in the process of planning. Planning itself consists of many tasks.

Mind mapping, grouping, citation, creating outlines, note-taking, brainstorming, looping, generating ideas, understanding the ideas of others, data collection, task analysis, audience analysis, researching, concept mapping, empathy mapping etc.

2. Drafting- You should spend 20% of your writing time to pen down all your ideas and findings on paper without worrying about the style, sequence or grammar choice.

At this point, it's always recommended to keep the perfectionist in your mind shut. Don't pay attention on the word choice, punctuation or even flow of writing, just keep on writing whatever ideas pop up into your head.

3. Revision- Now comes the most important part of your writing i.e. Revising, which consists of editing, omission, proof-reading. This part demands 50% of your time. So, plan this time into your writing deadlines to ensure there's space to let it rest.

Here, you finally look for the most appropriate format, style and tone of the writing to suit the purpose of writing.

Here, you need to ensure that your writing is not disjointed or disoriented it should flow naturally from known to unknown and familiar to unfamiliar (read chapter- "Perfectly Knitted Sentences"). Also, the correctness of data as well as grammar structures are to be focused here. In short, you need to polish your writing here. Following are few tips on how to revise your content-

I. Let the work breathe for a day- To revise a content, it's always best to let your work breathe for a day. Because, then only your mind will be able to read what's really there on the paper, rather than what you brain wants to see.

For example- Read it

I love cholocates!

Now again read it… This is what I mean.

II. Analyze audio version of your work- This works perfectly fine when you have no time to let your work rest for a while. By taking support from the ears, and listening the content aloud, the brain is less likely to fill in the gaps or automatically correct things. Moreover, if something sounds awkward or pretentious to you, might sound off to your potential customers too. Your content should sound smooth. If you find yourself stammering through poorly worded sentences, you better need to reframe your sentences.

III. KISS- Keep your sentences short and simple. During the writing process its very natural to use jargons or write long sentences. But while editing your content, limit industry specific language, and break long sentences into clear, simple points. There is nothing more frustrating than to having to read something thrice to understand it. Human brain looks for natural breaks while reading the text and uses those pauses to interpret what it's just read.

IV. Paragraph Splitting- How to edit your content also depends on the time available. If you have sufficient time then you should surely opt for Paragraph-Splitting method where you split your paragraph into sentences so as to analyze each sentence for its clarity as well as its flow with the preceding and following sentences.

V. A Quick Tip- Use **Grammarly proofreading tool** to find mistakes. I strongly recommend this tool when it comes to edit your own content. Grammarly automatically detects potential grammar, spelling, punctuation, word choice, tone and style mistakes such as double negatives, run-on sentences, and dangling modifiers in writing, following standard linguistic prescription. After you have used Grammarly a few times, you'll start recognizing common weaknesses in your own writing.

Now, a very important thing here is that this process of 30-20-50 writing doesn't follow a well-defined chronological order. The process is iterative, you may require to come back to planning stage while drafting. You may require to come back to planning stage even when you are editing your content to do additional research, adjust your focus, or reorganize ideas to create a more logical flow.

IV

TONE

In this digital era, every other day we get into the dire need of writing mails for official reasons, complaints, formal invitation, formal gratitude and so on. However, despite being very good at speaking, many of us feel burdened when it comes to writing. The reason behind this is that we can very well express our anger or gratitude towards someone with our frown or humble smile, but how to do it while writing?

So, the answer is - 'through the conscious selection of beginning line and ending line of the mail/letters'. Because these lines actually set the tone of your writing.

Mostly, the workplace writings take the neutral tone as they are meant for a variety of audience. But, many a times, the tone has to be set purposely suiting the requirement like if you have to write a complaint letter against a poor service which has caused your organization a very serious harm. Then obviously your tone needs to be a bit harsh so as to build pressure on the faulty system to fix the things as soon as possible. If, the management has to solicit or congratulate the employees on the successful completion of an ongoing project, obviously, the tone needs to be pleasant and joyful. In case of an immediate urgency, your tone needs to be a bit thoughtful. If you want to issue a warning letter, the tone also has to suit the purpose. So, let's go deep into it-

Neutral tone- for writing in a neutral tone, the words like apprise, inform, deliver, suggest and enquire etc. are to be used.

e.g. *"Kindly be apprised that an orientation programme is organized on 14th September, 20XX…….."*

"Kindly be notified about………..."

"You are hereby informed that…………"

"This is to enquire about……………"

"I humbly request you to kindly cooperate with us……….. (requesting)"

Emotional tone- For writing a letter to your client or any employee to express your feelings over any kind of loss occurred to them. The beginning like-

"It's sad to hear…."

"It's a matter of sorrow that………"

"I express my utter sorrow over…."

"It's really very unfortunate to hear about…."

Angry/discontent/frustrated tone- In case if you have to display your utter dissatisfaction over your employee at something which has caused you serious loss or might even have tarnished the goodwill of your organization, or in case if you are a customer and you realize that you are cheated and thus, you want financial compensation then obviously your tone needs to be a bit angry tone.

e.g.

"I regret to inform you that your staff needs training on dealing with customers……." *(Dissatisfaction)*

"With great dissatisfaction, I am bound to bring to your notice that..". (Angry)

"Despite several reminders, it has been observed that you are either ignoring our pleas or inviting some legal proceedings to mend your ways." *(angry)*

"With regret, I am bound to bring to your knowledge about the casual and indifferent attitude of your Maintenance dept. towards us, which in turn has caused a great inconvenience to us." *(dissatisfaction)*

"Owing to the repeatedly delays, we are now left with no other option than to consider legal proceedings against you." (angry)

Similarly, it's equally important to close the letter in an appropriate tone so as to get your message delivered exactly the way you want. Here are few examples-

"This kind of unprofessional attitude brings a bad name to your reputed organization." (angry)

"A dissatisfied customer is a clear red signal for the growth of any organization." (angry)

"What should a customer expect in return of paying maintenance?" (angry)

"What should a customer expect while buying 'X' from a renowned and well reputed brand name '............'?" (angry)

"This kind of indifference does not define the professionalism at all and it also tarnishes the Goodwill of any organization." (angry)

"I would welcome the opportunity to discuss matter further and to learn of how you propose to prevent a similar situation from recurring even in future." (discontent)

"Now as a customer I expect the higher authorities to intervene and put the system in place." (discontent)

Anxious tone- In case, your dealings with a client is on the verge of getting cancelled due to a situation which is not under your control, or if you can clearly see the impending loss and need to apprise your employees about it, obviously your tone needs to be either highly motivating so as to boost the morale of your employees or if the misfortune is certain then surely your tone needs to be anxious.

Pleasant tone- Your tone needs to convey your happy feelings on the occasions when it is expected of you. For a business relationship to last long, or when you might intentionally want your clients to be reminded of your existence on Earth, it's very important to greet your business friends on festivals or happy days. This is where your tone should be pleasant. Like-

"Greetings of the day on behalf of …………"

"On this very fortunate occasion of……., I want to convey my best wishes to you and your family…"

"Kindly accept my heartfelt wishes on this happy occasion of……"

And many more, so readers, no matter what state of mind you want your letter/mail to reflect- be it curt or polite, the right selection of words and expressions would surely serve you.

Just sit back and imagine yourself physically going to the service provider and shouting your heart out. Now just pen down/ type all your thoughts coated in a formal language and there you go.

V

PERFECTLY KNITTED SENTENCES

Okay, my dear reader, so until now we've seen how keeping sentences simple and concise helps readers comprehend your message clearly but is this only enough to keep your readers at ease?

No, there is one more way to make your readers comfortable with your writing and that is how logically as well as sequentially you knit your sentences altogether. To make it simpler, I would say how each sentence of your writing follows on to its preceding one.

To understand better, observe these two paragraphs-

Read the first paragraph-

Lactic acid-producing bacteria in the milk ferments and makes Buttermilk. When the milk is left to sit for a period of time to allow the cream and milk to separate, this fermentation occurs. Buttermilk contains vitamins, potassium, calcium and traces of phosphorus. Basically, it is common in warm climates, where unrefrigerated fresh milk sours quickly.

So, it was all informative and the content was also relevant. But still, reading it something was felt amiss.

Did you feel that the paragraph was a bit disjointed or disoriented? I personally feel that the sentences were not interconnected, they bounced and jumped a lot.

Now read the second paragraph-

Buttermilk is a fermented dairy liquid left over from churning butter from cultured or fermented milk. This fermentation is common in warm climates, where unrefrigerated fresh milk sours quickly. During this time when the milk gets sour, naturally occurring lactic acid-producing bacteria in the milk ferments it. Because of this fermentation, Buttermilk contains vitamins, potassium, calcium and traces of phosphorus.

Okay, so both these paragraphs contained same content, same vocabulary, equally technical language, still the second paragraph is more composed and it also facilitates the reader to comprehend the content easily.

So, let us split the paragraph into sentences to understand better (which we call as paragraph splitting)-

Opening sentences of both the paragraphs-

    i.   *Lactic acid-producing bacteria in the milk ferments and makes Buttermilk.*

    ii.   *Buttermilk is a fermented dairy liquid left over from churning butter from cultured or fermented milk.*

As a reader seeking information about Buttermilk, you might get a bit confused when you start reading about lactic acid or fermentation etc. So, it's better to start with the information, the reader is already familiar with i.e. buttermilk. As a reader, you might not be aware of it's composition or benefits but at least you are aware that the term buttermilk exists. So, it doesn't give you cognitive load and you feel at ease.

Let us proceed-

    I.   *When the milk is left to sit for a period of time to allow the cream and milk to separate, this fermentation occurs.*

    II.   *This fermentation is common in warm climates, where unrefrigerated fresh milk sours quickly.*

Now, you see that in the second line of first paragraph, the fact about 'letting the milk sit' comes out of nowhere. The reader is left baffled. Instead, in the second paragraph, the thread is picked up naturally from where it was left in the first line i.e. fermented milk. So now, it goes on elaborating the fermentation.

So, the reader is gliding through gently from known to unknown and the sentence is following the previous sentence and weaving the threads. And thus, you seem to find a knitted piece of writing.

Third sentence of both the paragraphs-

i. *Buttermilk contains vitamins, potassium, calcium and traces of phosphorus.*

ii. *During this time when the milk gets sour, naturally occurring lactic acid-producing bacteria in the milk ferments it.*

So, here again you can easily observe the flow of sentences in both the paragraphs and thus, you can compare both the paragraphs and understand how to write a tightly knitted piece of writing by gradually shifting from known to unknown, familiar to unfamiliar and trying to pick the ideas from the end of the preceding sentences to frame the beginning of each consecutive sentence.

VI

CLARITY OF SENTENCES

For a piece of writing to be clear and concise, it needs to avoid ambiguity. Read further to know how to do it-

The verb should not be so far from the subject as it creates a lot of cognitive load on readers' minds keeping all the information in their heads before they finally reach the verb. For example-

*"A long sentence, in which the writer delays the core to the middle of the sentence or in which the core is broken up so readers have to remember how the sentence started, **is difficult to read."***

Now read the easier variant with the whole core at the start-

*"A **long sentence becomes difficult** to read when you delay the core until the middle of the sentence or when you break up the core."*

Even grammatically correct sentences can sometimes be very confusing. Thus, while framing

the sentences it should always be ensured that the sentences should not be ambiguous like read the following sentence and try to comprehend-

The complex houses married and single soldiers and their families.

The given sentence is grammatically correct but still it is not easy to understand. Reading it for the first time, the reader will get confused. In this sentence, 'complex' doesn't serve as adjective but as a noun i.e. the 'housing complex', 'houses' is a verb instead of noun and 'married' is an adjective instead of verb.

So, only being grammatically correct doesn't guarantee that your writing is appropriate.

Last but not the least, try to keep your sentences short.

VII

PERSUASION TECHNIQUES

No matter what business you deal with or whichever field you are associated with, you get into the need of writing to convince or persuade people for a certain scheme/belief daily. So, this section deals with the persuasion techniques.

Let us begin with various modes of persuasion- Ethos, Pathos and Logos.

First of all, as we see the overall rhetoric situation of a persuasive communication, we see three main components- Writer/speaker, Text and Reader/listener.

Ethos is all about the credibility of the writer/speaker. Logo is much more related to the logic, the logical reasoning behind your argument in the text. Pathos is the appeal to the emotion of the reader.

So, the following diagram makes it easy to understand and remember.

Speaker/Writer	Content/Text	Audience/Reader
• ETHOS	• LOGOS	• PATHOS
• Related to the reputation of the writer/speaker	• Related to the logical arguments given in the text	• Appeal to the emotion/feelings of audience/reader

The following examples will help you understand it better-

Look at the following advertisements-

What did you observe? Why do advertisements need doctors/celebrities to prove their statements?

What impression do these advertisements leave on us as an end user?

Our mind starts believing on these products because of the reputation of these personalities. So, when you use credentials, certificates, reputation, credibility or knowledge of a writer or speaker to promote an idea, it is an appeal to ethos. The ethics of the presenter is put to use to compel the end user to believe in what is said. Most of the other advertisements, where famous celebrities or sports personalities are shown using any product and speaking high about those products, also use this mode of persuasion.

Now look at these examples-

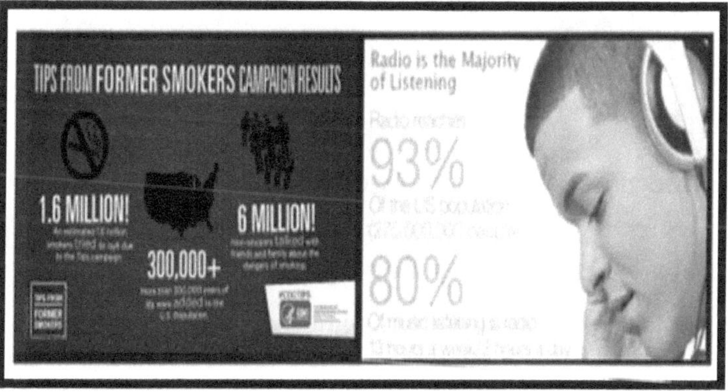

What do you feel these advertisements are doing?

Why do these advertisements use statistics, data or numbers to prove their statements?

What impression do these advertisements leave on us?

We start believing on these logical statements. Yes, the logical arguments put forward to prove any point is actually termed as an appeal to logos.

Now look at these advertisements-

Didn't it affect you? These advertisements directly knock at your heart and thus, arouse strong feelings or emotions which in turn make you believe in what is being said/shown to you.

This is an appeal to pathos.

Thus, a good mix of all these appeals will work miraculously for you when it comes to persuasion.

Now if you are an enthusiast who writes about the problems prevailing in the society in forms of articles or blogs, you need to structure your content in the following way-

- First you need to introduce the issue/problem to your readers along with your urge to write about it like why you intend to write over this issue and to what extent do you feel that this issue needs to be addressed.
- Next you develop your writing with the causes behind the issue/problem.
- Then you gradually shift your ideas towards the effect/impact of the problem on you, the society as well as the country or if it is a matter of interest for the entire world, you must focus on the impact on the world.
- Now, suggest some solutions or recommendation for the problem as it will then only be worthwhile for your readers to have gone through it.
- Now conclude your points in the last stanza along with reiterating the main point you started your article with.

POETRY: A GLIMPSE

Always be a poet, even in prose."

--*Charles Baudelaire*

Poetry: A Glimpse
(Equally useful for poets and prose writers)

I can see a swathe of puzzled faces…

Baffled to read the heading? How can this section be useful for a story writer?

Okay…

Read to know the idea behind it…

Poetry.. The word itself **arises** a strong emotion in the heart of a poetry lover.

Poetry writing is so intrigued in itself. It's the most wild and free kind of writing because it's derived from emotions and imagination. The wildest imagination produces the most liberated lines. On the other hand, poetry is all full of forms, and rules, and rhythms and meters and syllables. So, it's quite baffling.

Let me clear this clutter... Alright, so the first thing is that poetry is all about the spontaneous flow of the inner feelings. The poets have got all the freedom to express their feelings in the form they want. But the more freedom, the more chaos. What happens if you leave a wild bull in the busy marketplace. Our imaginations are no less wild than anything in the world. So, don't you think these imaginations or emotions need some guideposts? So, there comes the role of rules. Because no doubt that the poets have got the poetic license to break the rules but I think breaking the rules becomes more impactful if we are fully aware of those rules. And who knows, these rules might also work as guideposts for us… So, you are first recommended to get acquainted with the structure of various types of poems and the poetic devices too.

So, as I said in the heading that **it's equally useful for the prose writers to read this article because poetry is concise and impactful. It uses strong language, and no more words than necessary. If you know how to write a poem, your prose will become crunchier and more impactful. So, eliminate all the unnecessary words or phrases and make every word count.**

Poetry actually uses images and sounds more than mere words. Thus, the poets make the readers travel into the whole new world of experience. Read the following two lines-

She was happy

The smiles of her dark-blue eyes sparkled like the sea when first lighted up by the rays of the sun.

In the abovementioned lines, the first line told us something, but the second line showed an image to us. This is the beauty of poems.

Now read the following line-

"Her smile spread like red tint on ripening tomatoes."

The first line talked about happiness which is an abstract idea. It is a word that can only refer to a concept or feeling- it's not a concrete, tangible thing. Some other examples of abstract ideas are love, liberty, marriage, courage etc. These abstract ideas have different meanings for different persons. Thus, these words make your poem weak. In place of using these abstractions, you can think of the similar images or concrete objects to convey that emotion or concept. Like-

Freedom – An abstract idea

Breaking barriers, swinging high, birds flying freely – concrete

Love- An abstract idea

The sudden gust of wind at the sight of your beloved, cuddling your baby, petting your pet – concrete

Courage – An abstract idea

Looking straight into the eyes – concrete

Thus, the main thing is to make your readers see through your mind and hear through your ears to get the real emotions. And making your readers indulge into your poem is only possible when you yourself indulge into it. Many a times it happens that we spend hours, days, weeks, months or even years to start writing just because we don't seem to find that **PERFECT** topic to write about. And ironically that **PERFECT** topic never comes to our mind. Because that **PERFECT** idea or topic seems to reside in that ideal state of our Physics books, which actually does not exist. So, **instead of chasing some dramatic, grand emotion to write about, try to find some ordinary concrete thing from day to day life which makes us all human.** It can be anything as small as an ant taking food to its anthill, the old plastic outdoor chair faded by the sun or as massive as gray distant clouds slowly swirling.

So, just start composing your poetry on whatever is around you right now.

You don't start out writing good stuff. You start out writing crap and thinking its good stuff, and then gradually you get better at it.

That's why I say one of the most valuable traits is persistence."

— Octavia E. Butler

Obviously, it's not that one day you will wake up and become a writer. You need to try your hands on it. Just like any other skill, writing is also best learnt through practice. Many a times, what we start writing with, end up with entirely changed ideology. It happens because until you start working on anything, you won't get the required clarity onto that. We learn through the process. Many of us feel scared of starting/venturing something new with a concern that we don't have the required expertise on it. Actually, what happens, when you start a new work you become an expert by the time your work is accomplished. So never wait for **THE** excellent point of time to start writing when you **THINK** you'll master the subject. Rather, master the subject by writing on it with great dedication and devotion.

⌁

www.ingramcontent.com/pod-product-compliance
Lightning Source LLC
Chambersburg PA
CBHW051902130726
47987CB00002B/942